The Last of the Fianna

Also by Michael Scott

The Children of Lir

MICHAEL SCOTT

The Last
of the Fianna

An Irish Legend

Illustrated by Gary Ward

A Pied Piper Book
Methuen Children's Books

For Piers,
a book of his own

First published 1987
by Methuen Children's Books Ltd
11 New Fetter Lane, London EC4P 4EE
Text copyright © 1987 Michael Scott
Illustrations copyright © 1987 Gary Ward
Cover illustration copyright © 1987 Jim Fitzpatrick
Printed in Great Britain by
St Edmundsbury Press Ltd, Bury St Edmunds, Suffolk

British Library Cataloguing-in-Publication Data

Scott, Michael, *1959*–
    The last of the fianna.,—(Pied piper)
    I. Title   II. Ward, Gary
    823'.914[J]   PZ7

    ISBN 0–416–95920–2

'I was in Tir na nOg, the Land of Youth, when I was a boy. I met Oisin, Prince of the Fianna, last of the old Heroes of Ireland. I was with him when he returned to Ireland.

'You don't believe me? Well then, let me tell you about Oisin, and Niamh Golden-Hair, and their daughter Plure and the land of Tir na nOg.

'And let me tell you about the small part I played in his return from the magical land.

'My name is Colum . . .'

Chapter One

The White Horse

The small boy's name was Colum, and he was lost in the forest. It was late and he was cold and tired, his legs ached and, like his bare arms, they were scratched from the nettles and brambles. He leaned against a tree, breathing deeply, wondering what he should do. He had tried shouting, but there had been no answer and the forest was so big and dark, it only seemed to swallow the sound, and turn his shout into a whisper. All that was left for him to do now was to pray for help.

But to which gods? His mother and father followed two different gods; the old Celtic Gods and the new Christian faith.

Then he had an idea – he would pray to both, and he would follow whichever god helped him find his way back home. He straightened up and brushed leaves and twigs from his short tunic.

'My name is Colum, son of King Laoighre,' he began, his voice sounding very loud in the silence. 'I am lost in this forest – and I want to go home!' His voice shook towards the end, and he had to take a deep breath to finish, as he called upon the old Celtic gods. 'Dagda and Danu and fair Angus, help me now.'

He waited for a little while, watching the moths flittering white and silver in the moonbeams, and then, when nothing seemed to be happening, he tried again.

'My name is Colum, son of Queen Angras, who is a follower of the White Christ and His teachings. Will you help me find my way out of this forest?'

In the depth of the forest, something cracked loudly; Colum's heart leapt and thumped painfully. He heard a whispering fluttering sound and then something brushed past his face on feather-soft wings, and he saw huge eyes glowing yellow white in the moonlight as they flashed past. He stumbled backwards, caught his heel on a root and fell over, but he realized it was only an owl hunting for its evening meal. His own stomach rumbled then, reminding him just how hungry he was. It had been a long time since he had last eaten.

He climbed to his feet – and then he saw a shining, sparkling white spot through the trees. He felt his head begin to pound and he

swallowed hard. He parted some leaves and peered through the dark branches, turning his head from side to side, trying to make out the shining shape. But then he took a deep breath – after all, he had asked for help, hadn't he, and he wasn't afraid, was he? He took a step forward, and then another and then another, moving towards the shape.

Leaves crackled and rustled, like people whispering and muttering together, but the closer he seemed to come to the white spot, the further away it seemed to move. It made no sound as it slipped through the trees, and with the shifting shapes and tall trees and branches, Colum still couldn't make out what he was seeing.

Soon he was running through the trees and bushes, with only the pale light of the now sinking moon to guide him. All his fear and terror were forgotten, all he wanted to do now was to catch up with the white shape – whatever it was.

Colum crashed out of the forest and stumbled and fell. He lay on the ground panting hard, while his legs felt rubbery, and his throat and chest burned. He pushed himself upwards, and then he realized that there was sand under his hands. He looked at it in shock: he must have run for miles!

He sat up and sure enough, ahead of him was a broad sandy beach, with the sand now black and silver in the moonlight, and the ocean all polished blackness in the night.

A shadow moved on the beach and he jumped with fright.

And then a horse stepped out from behind a rock. A tall silver-white horse.

Colum stood up slowly, not wishing to frighten the animal. He waited, but the creature didn't move, and then he walked down the beach towards it. His legs still felt a bit shaky, but his breathing was now back to normal. However, he knew that he could not walk home tonight, he was far too tired. But if he had a horse, it would be different. All he had to do was to ride northwards until he reached the tall Cliffs of Moher and then cut eastward across the country. He knew his home was somewhere to the east.

But first he had to catch the horse.

The moon came out from behind a cloud and bathed the creature in silver light, so that it sparkled and shimmered brilliantly. It was a beautifully tall and slender animal, with an erect head, bright intelligent eyes and a long flowing mane and tail. Perhaps the head was a little too thin, and the ears a little too long and pointed and perhaps the hooves were a little too slender, but Colum didn't notice those things. All he saw was the most magnificent animal in the world. His father owned some lovely horses, and he had seen some of the horses of the Iron Legioneers from the Land of the Britons, but this animal was nothing like theirs. In fact, it was like nothing he had ever seen before.

The horse stood quite still while the young boy approached, only lowering its finely-boned

head to stare with huge unblinking eyes at him. Once, its foreleg struck the sand, splashing in the foaming shallows, the water sparkling brightly.

'Easy . . . easy now . . . easy. . . .' Colum spoke softly and gently, in the same tone of voice he had heard his father's horsemen talk to the animals in the stables behind the palace at Tara. He stroked its smooth white skin. It felt like polished metal beneath his fingers, and its thick silver mane felt like threads of silk.

He stood for a moment looking up at the horse, wondering what to do. There was something mysterious and a little frightening about the horse and, if it had been sent in answer to his prayers, which god had sent it – the old pagan gods, or the new Christian ones? And if he climbed up on to its slender back, would he be able to control it. . . ? And if he couldn't control it, where would it take him?

But he was so far from home, too far to walk. There was no other way.

Colum gripped the mane tightly in both hands and then quickly pulled himself up on to the creature's back. He sat there, holding tightly on to the mane, expecting the horse to buck and jump around, trying to throw him off. But the horse stood patient and unmoving.

When he was comfortable, Colum kicked his heels lightly against its flanks and pulled at the mane. 'Come on boy, let's go.'

The horse didn't move.

Colum kicked his heels again. 'Come on, come on,' he urged.

The horse swung its head around and stared at the boy for a few heartbeats with its huge eyes. Colum smiled to himself; the horse looked very intelligent – almost too intelligent to be a horse. It blinked slowly, and then Colum suddenly realized that its eyes were slit-pupilled like a cat's, and not round, as a horse's should be. Suddenly he knew that the old Celtic gods had sent him a fairy horse. He was frightened now. He knew what happened to people who rode the moon-silver steeds of the fairy folk – they were usually never heard of again. He was about to climb down when the animal suddenly moved.

It turned, its shining silver hooves splashing noisily through the shallows, and then it faced out towards the open sea. 'Stop . . . please stop.' Colum pulled on the creature's mane, but it only seemed to spur it on to a gallop. Soon the water was up to its fetlocks, and tall sheets of water splashed up and over its glowing body and the terrified boy.

'I'll let go and fall off,' Colum thought, as the horse continued to gallop straight into the sea. He was about to let go when he felt his skin tingle with a warm glow, and then he felt the horse's body burning beneath his legs. It seemed to shift then, to move, and it slowly came up out of the water as if it weighed no more than a piece of rotten wood. Colum looked down in amazement: the horse was galloping on the water, its hooves barely breaking the surface!

He looked back, but already the beach was a thin black line, far, far away — and ahead of him lay nothing but the open sea.

Chapter Two

The Island

Colum must have slept at some time during the night, although he couldn't actually remember drifting off to sleep, nor could he remember how he had managed to stay on the horse all that time. He remembered awakening.

He found himself sitting up straight on the broad back of the white horse with the sun rising behind him, sending a long thin shadow straight out before him across the dark, white-capped waves. Overhead, where the sun had washed the night from the sky, the heavens were a pale blue, but in front of him night still lingered, although it had paled to a light purple and only the brightest stars remained visible.

Colum looked up into the sky and tried to remember their names ... and then he was wide awake: the stars in the sky had changed, they were not the stars he knew!

All his fears and terrors came back. He looked around frantically, but there was nothing to be seen except the sea stretching in all directions, broad and flat and grey with nothing but a thin band of cloud on the horizon. 'Help!' he shouted, but the fairy horse twisted its thin head and looked back at him. It bared its large, flat, yellow teeth and brought them together with a click. It was a warning, Colum decided.

The young boy took a deep breath, and forced himself to stay calm. There were tears behind his eyes and he could feel his throat burning – but he wasn't going to cry. Not yet, anyway. He looked around again, finally coming back to the only thing he could see and that was the clouds. He squinted his eyes half-closed and looked again; those clouds seemed strange, they were too low and flat and regular in shape. They might be an island or islands. Another few moments and the sky would be clear and he would know for sure.

Colum forced himself to stare down at the horse's mane and think carefully. As far as he could remember there should be no islands ahead of him. He had set out with the sun sinking in front of him – which was the west – and now it was rising behind him – which was the east. Therefore he had been travelling in a straight line for most of the night on the back of this strange horse-creature, and therefore there should be no islands out here in the broad Western Ocean. He took a deep breath and looked up.

There was an island ahead of him.

The sky had brightened to a pale eggshell blue over the land and, although it was still dark and shadowed at this distance, something on it caught the sunlight and reflected it back in a bright golden light. As Colum watched, and the sun rose higher in the heavens, most of the island began to glow and shimmer and sparkle with rainbow colours, until it was just a mass of shifting colours and he could no longer bear to look at it.

He touched the lucky stone with the hole in it, which he wore around his neck on a leather string, and wished he was back in Erin in his own bed in the palace at Tara. 'Maybe it's a dream,' he thought, but then salty ice-cold water splashed up into his face and he knew it was no dream.

The horse continued to gallop on – straight into the rainbow lights which now seemed to have spread all across the surface of the water and the sky ahead of him. The lights hurt his eyes and he closed them against the glare. . . .

18

Colum awoke again when he felt the horse's body begin to tingle and grow warm beneath his numb thighs and calves, and then he felt the horse shift and move downwards. The boy came fully awake when he heard the silver hooves strike sparks from a rough stony beach. He realized that he must have dozed again for some time, and he also discovered that he was very, very hungry. Even as he thought about it, his stomach rumbled and growled.

However, all that was forgotten as the horse began to splash through shallow rock-pools and up along the beach. Ahead of him stretched a rough stony shore which spread out on to a broad golden-sanded beach that led upwards to a lush, evergreen jungle. The horse delicately picked its way up the beach and pushed into the forest.

Colum had never seen such trees or plants before: they rose up into the sky in tall wooden pillars without a trace of stem or twig or branch until they neared the top and then they seemed to burst into leaf and branch. Brightly coloured flowers were twisted on vines around the bases of the tall trees. They were every colour and shape imaginable. He saw star-shaped flowers, trumpet-shapes, shield-shapes, sword-shapes

19

and even one that opened when Colum neared it and then turned and swivelled to follow him as he passed.

He shivered, but not with the cold, rather with excitement. His large green eyes opened wide in astonishment as he looked around.

The horse continued up along a thin pathway that was lined with strange and curious bushes. Some were small and squat with thick, rubbery leaves; others were tall and thin with long sharp-edged leaves and long thorns, while still others, which seemed a mixture of two or three bushes, were shaped like men or animals.

There were creatures too in this strange forest. Colum saw huge winged butterflies spiralling from flower to flower, or resting in a broad, living carpet of colour on a bush. He saw birds, some small and quick and drab-coloured, others large and slow and brightly feathered. He saw one bird which was so beautiful that it took his breath away; it was tall and thin, with a squat body and a long slender head and it poised on one stick-like leg in a small slow-moving river. It was bright pink in colour.

Larger animals moved through this forest also. He saw huge cats, far, far bigger than the cats that scavenged around the kitchens at Tara.

Some were striped in black and gold, whilst others were spotted with black or dark-brown spots on a bronze-coloured body.

And there were unicorns also.

One stepped out into the track and stood staring at him with huge intelligent eyes, its spiralled horn almost crystal clear and reflecting the green tinge of the forest. It hesitated a moment and then turned and leaped like a deer into the undergrowth and was gone, with barely a rustle of leaves.

And it was when he saw the unicorn that Colum knew for certain where he was.

The track opened out into a clearing surrounded by trees and, in the centre of the clearing was a tall slender tower rising straight up into the sky.

The horse stopped and turned its head around to stare at Colum with its cat's eyes.

'You want me to get down, don't you?' he asked.

The horse continued to look at him without blinking.

'Yes, I think you do,' Colum answered himself, surprised to find that his own voice wasn't shaking too much. The terrifying horse and the wild ride across the water and now this strange and beautiful island had frightened him so much . . . that he was no longer afraid. He swung his leg over the creature's back and dropped lightly to the ground. He groaned aloud as his aching legs began to throb with pins and needles, and he knelt on the soft grass to rub them. When he looked up the horse was gone and he was alone in the clearing.

When his legs had stopped tingling, Colum stood up and walked towards the tower. He ran his hand down the smooth metal; it seemed to be made from solid silver, and as he looked up its shining length he noticed that there were no windows and, except for the tall arched doorway before him, there seemed to be no other opening in it.

He stood outside the open doorway, wondering what to do. 'Should I go in?' he asked himself aloud.

'You are very welcome to do so.'

A tall, slim woman stepped into the doorway before Colum. She was very, very beautiful, with a small, almost triangular face and large green eyes.

Colum gazed at her in astonishment; he had never seen anyone like her before in his life. She stepped forward out into the full daylight and Colum saw that what he had taken for a headdress of some sort was actually her hair, and as she moved, it whispered softly to itself. Her hair was the colour of freshly-made butter, and flowed in a pale yellow band down her back to just below her knees. It seemed to hold the light and then reflect it back again and, against the bright red dress with the green trim which she was wearing, the effect was breathtaking.

'I've been expecting you,' the woman said softly, in a strange, almost musical accent.

'Expecting me?' Colum said slowly, still staring at the woman open-mouthed. 'How?'

'When Bainte goes into the World of Men he always brings us back a . . . visitor,' she smiled. 'I knew he would bring someone.'

'Bainte?' Colum asked.

'The White Horse. I am Niamh Golden-Hair,' she continued, her voice as lovely as a song. 'Will you come with me, please?'

Without waiting for a reply, she turned and disappeared into the tower. Colum hesitated for a few moments, feeling his heart begin to pound in his chest, but then, realizing that there was little else he could do, followed the golden-haired woman into the tower.

He stopped in amazement just inside the door. The tower itself was perfectly empty, with only a spiral staircase running up along the inside of the wall, but what amazed Colum was that there was light coming in through the walls which was shifting and curling and moving all about him like smoke. He saw a flash of red out of the corner of his eye as Niamh moved slowly and silently up the stairs and he turned to follow her.

He found that the stairs seemed to go on forever, winding upwards and upwards. Although they were broad, they were quite big and he had to stretch to bring his feet up to the next one

25

and by the time he reached the top he was quite exhausted.

Indeed, he had been concentrating so much on the next step . . . and the next step . . . and the next step . . . that he was quite surprised when he suddenly stepped out into the sunlight.

He found himself on top of the tower, with a scented breeze whipping in off the ocean and cooling him down. A man turned around to face him, a huge, muscular, red-haired and red-bearded man, dressed in a brown and gold jerkin and a pale gold cloak. His eyes were grey and piercing, but his smile was kindly.

The woman stood beside the man and linked her arm with his. 'This is my husband, Oisin,' she said slowly.

'Then this is Tir na nOg!' Colum exclaimed. 'The land of the Ever Young, the Fairy Land!'

Chapter Three

The Warrior

The tall red-haired and bearded warrior and the young red-haired and freckle-faced boy might have been father and son, for both in looks and colouring they were very similar. Niamh looked from one to the other and then she slipped her arm free of her husband's.

'I will return shortly,' she said quietly, looking hard at Colum. Something in her eyes frightened the boy, and when she looked from him to Oisin, Colum saw what looked like anger — or fear — in her face. She gave a short bow and then disappeared silently through the arched doorway and down the stairs.

Oisin and Colum bowed courteously to her as she left and then turned back to face each other. They stood looking at each other in silence for a few moments, and then the warrior spread out both hands. 'How did you know this place?' he asked softly.

Colum smiled shyly. 'I only guessed at first,

but then when Niamh told me your name, I knew this must be Tir na nOg. All Erin knows the tale of Oisin, son of Finn, who went to the magical Isle of Youth and never returned.'

'I will return some day,' Oisin said quickly. 'And soon,' he added, turning around and leaning across the battlements to stare out over the isle and towards the thin blue thread of the sea that could be seen in the distance.

Colum joined him and peered over the top of the wall. But it was just a little too high and he could barely see the distant blue line. 'Let me,' Oisin said and, with one hand, lifted the boy as easily as if he weighed no more than a handful of leaves. He set him down on top of the wall's tooth-like stones – the merlons – and held him with a hand through his belt.

The view from the top of the tower was breath-taking. Colum looked down first – and then wished he hadn't: it was a long, long way to the ground. He swayed dizzily, but Oisin tightened his grip on the belt. 'I won't let you fall,' he said reassuringly.

Colum swallowed hard and opened his eyes, which he had squeezed shut. The trees flowed away from the tower in a broad blanket of green; some he knew – oak, ash, elm and chestnut, but others were strange to him. They were every shade and variation of green; some were so light that they might have been golden-green, while others were so dark that they were almost black.

He suddenly blinked and looked again. Perhaps it was his imagination, but surely he could see a pattern, a design, picked out in the different colours? A shape, a curious twisting, curling shape, with the dark-leaved trees on the outside of the circle, and then the trees with lighter coloured leaves in near the centre of the grove.

He turned around to ask Oisin about the pattern, and then his gaze fell on the golden brooch the warrior was wearing on his shoulder, pinning his cloak. It was a beautiful, delicate piece of work – and it was the same design that was picked out in the trees below.

Oisin saw him looking at it and touched it with his fingertips. 'It was a present from Niamh,' he said. 'She is of the race of the Tuatha De Danann; it was they who introduced metal-working into Eriu. They are the finest gold and silver smiths in all the known world.'

'But the trees . . .' Colum pointed down.

The tall warrior nodded. 'The circle and this

design,' he touched the brooch again, 'is a very special and powerful talisman for the De Danann,' he explained. 'This talisman – which is a charm, a magical charm – keeps this island safe and protected.' He suddenly hoisted Colum on to his broad shoulders and walked around the battlements. 'Look; the entire island is circular, the palaces are circular and, although you cannot see it from here, the reef that guards the beaches is circular also. And all of them have this design on them,' he added, putting the young boy down.

'A magical island,' Colum said to himself.

Oisin nodded seriously. 'A magical island.' He moved to the door and took the first few steps before he turned around and reached out his hand for Colum's. 'Come, and I will show you this magical island.'

Colum slipped his hand into Oisin's and followed him down the broad steps. Strangely, he wasn't frightened now. As long as he stayed close to Oisin, he knew he would be safe, because Oisin was human too – he wouldn't let the fairy folk harm another human.

As they climbed down the steps, Oisin told him a little about Tir na nOg, his voice echoing hollowly off the walls. 'This is a magical island,' he repeated. 'Here you will find creatures that have long since died out in our world: unicorns, dragons, flying lizards, the great long-toothed cat, the giant elk and many, many more. This world protects them, because you see, there is no time on this island.' He paused and looked over his shoulder at Colum who was still a step behind. 'The magical circle you saw protects us from time; that is why this place is called the Land of the Ever Young. There is no age and no death here.'

They had now reached the last of the steps and Colum called out for the warrior to stop for a bit while he sat down on the bottom step and tried to catch his breath. His stomach rumbled again and he looked up at Oisin. 'I'm very hungry,' he said.

The warrior smiled. 'Oh, but I'll soon attend to that.' He reached down and pulled Colum to his feet, and then, in one smooth movement, he hoisted him up on to his shoulders. 'Duck your head now,' he warned as they neared the doorway.

Outside, Oisin paused for a moment and breathed deeply. Colum took a deep breath also, and found that he could almost taste the air; it was fresh, sweet and smelt of cut grass.

'This way.' Oisin moved across the little glade and down a path almost directly opposite to the one Colum had used. The track was lined with tall, shining trees, and brought them deeper and deeper into the forest. It was quiet and peaceful, and felt . . . almost sleepy.

'What do you do all day?' Colum asked the warrior.

Oisin paused before answering, and then he shrugged, almost upsetting Colum off his shoulders. 'Oh, I do. . . .' He paused again, as if trying to remember just what he did. 'I hunt,' he said slowly, 'although naturally I don't kill the animals, I just track them to their lairs. I compose songs and Niamh is teaching me to play the harp. I've also taken up metal working, and I'm making myself a sword so that when I return to Eriu, it will be magical. . . .'

'Because you made it here,' Colum said quickly. 'Why do you keep calling Erin, Eriu?' he asked then.

'Erin?' Oisin said, puzzled.

'Yes, Erin, the name of my country,' Colum said.

'My country is called Eriu,' Oisin said slowly.

'It hasn't been called Eriu for many, many

years now. One of my father's druids, an old, old man, sometimes uses that name when he is teaching me history.'

'History?' Oisin whispered, suddenly feeling cold. He swung the young boy off his shoulders and set him down on his feet. He then knelt down and stared into Colum's soft grey eyes with his own grey-coloured, but harder eyes. 'Tell me, Colum, how many years have I been gone from Eriu . . . Erin?' His voice was low and intense, and his grip on Colum's arms tightened almost painfully. 'How long?'

Colum shook his head, puzzled. 'I don't know,' he said slowly, and then he winced as Oisin's grip tightened.

The warrior saw the pain in the boy's eyes and quickly released his hold. 'I'm sorry,' he said, 'I didn't mean to hurt.'

'It's been a long time,' Colum finished.

'Would it be three years . . . thirteen years . . . thirty years? Would it be thirty years?' he asked softly.

'It would be more I think,' the young boy answered. 'Long enough for you to have become a legend.'

Oisin bowed his head and squeezed his eyes shut. He should have known: there was no time on this island, and who knew exactly how many years had passed in Eriu?

And now he was a legend. Surely that meant that many, many years had passed?

But no, Oisin didn't want to believe that. He wouldn't believe it!

He opened his eyes suddenly. This boy had known him when they had first met; therefore he had not been forgotten – and surely if he had been missing for a long time, he would not be remembered? And then another thought struck him: his father, Finn, had been a legend in his own lifetime.

The tall warrior stood up and ran his fingers through his red hair. He looked down at the freckle-faced boy staring up at him and he made a decision: it was now time for him to return to Eriu. A brief visit, two days, perhaps three, just to see his family and his old friends, and then he would return. He had never felt the need to return to his homeland before, but now, looking down at the boy – a human boy, the first human he had seen in . . . well, in a long time – he felt very homesick.

'Come on.' He ruffled Colum's hair and took his hand and led him down a twisting side-path. 'We'll get you some food first,' he said.

The path led along an avenue lined with tall brightly-leaved bushes that twitched and turned to follow the two figures as they passed. At the end of the path, there was a small circular pool, and beside the pool was a round beehive-shaped hut with a single tree growing beside it.

'This is my forge,' Oisin explained, pointing to the stone building. 'Niamh suggested I set it up out here so that the hammering would not disturb any of the inhabitants of this isle – most of whom seem to spend all their time sleeping,' he added. 'Niamh tells me that they will awake and ride again, across the seas to Eriu, when the land is threatened.' He shrugged. 'Well, I don't know about that; if Eriu is threatened then my father and the knights of the Fianna can take care of it, I'm sure. Anyway, here's your food.' He reached up and pulled a brightly-coloured fruit from the branches of the tree and handed it to Colum.

The boy looked at it closcly. It was a large orange ball, with a pebbled skin and a tiny black star at one end. Colum turned it over and over in his hands, looking in wonder at its bright colour and feeling its strange texture. He had never seen anything like this.

'What is it called?' he asked Oisin.

The warrior took the fruit from his hand and, with his strong fingers showed the boy how to peel it. 'Apparently, this is a common fruit in the warm lands that lie far, far to the south of Eriu. It's a stranger to our land, but everything grows in Tir na nOg, and here the De Danann call it after its colour. They call it an Orange.' He broke the fruit into parts and handed it back to the boy.

Colum bit into one of the segments and tasted bitter-sweetness. The taste was strange and the odour of the juice was sharp and . . . he wasn't really sure whether he liked it or not. He took another bite, and wrinkled his nose as the juice spurted and tickled. He decided he liked it.

'Of course,' Oisin added, 'like everything else on this island, it is magical. You'll find you won't need to eat again today.'

And it was true; with one bite Colum's hunger vanished.

The young boy followed the warrior into the hut. It was dark, with the only light coming in through the open doorway, catching the highlights and glints of metal. Oisin moved about, and soon a fire began to crackle in the centre of the room. Colum saw the shadowy figure of Oisin set fire to a twig and then move around the small room, lighting small rush lights and oil bowls. When there was enough light to see by, he handed the glowing twig to Colum. 'Will you light the rest for me?'

Colum took the twig and cupped its smouldering end in his hand. If the lamps and lights were arranged as they were at home, they should be in the darkest corners, out of the way of draughts. He moved around slowly until he found a tall bundle of reeds tied together and stuck in a metal ring set into the wall. He blew on the end of the twig until it glowed red hot and touched its end to the dry reeds. Their tips must have been coated with fish oil because they blazed alight almost immediately.

Soon the room was ablaze with light, and then Colum looked around in wonder.

It was not unlike a forge he had once been in at home, except that this was so small, and unlike the other forge, which had old swords, broken wheels, odd lengths of rusted metal lying around, this was very neat — and all the metal here was gold and silver and shaped into armour and weapons of some kind.

There were helmets, both with horns and without; others with nose guards, others with ear flaps, others that covered the face completely.

There were spears, some short and thick, others long and thin. Shields, flat and tall, round and short, covered one wall. Just beside the door was a short mail shirt, each tiny and perfect link of chain made out of solid silver.

Oisin watched Colum's eyes opening wide, and he smiled. 'You might say that it's my hobby,' he said.

'There's one other piece,' Oisin said. He turned around and began to unwrap something from a piece of cloth on the bench behind him. 'It's strange that you've come here now,' he said. 'I always promised myself that I would return to Eriu when this was finished. It is just finished now.'

'What is it?' Colum asked in a whisper.

'It's a present for my father,' Oisin explained, unwinding a long strip of thick fleecy cloth.

'But Finn . . .' Colum began.

'He must be very disappointed with me,' Oisin said.

'Why?' Colum asked, immediately forgetting what he had been just about to say.

'Why?' Oisin sounded surprised. 'Why? Because I just left him that day long ago on the banks of the Lakes of Killarney.' He moved to the door of the hut and stepped outside. Colum followed him.

'What really happened that morning, Oisin?' he said.

Oisin looked down at him. He smiled and then gestured to the small lake and as they walked down to it, he finished unwrapping the long thin bundle.

Colum gasped. It was a sword; a long gleaming length of metal taller than himself. The blade was broad at the hilt and tapered to a fine point. The pommel and hilt – the handle – were of solid gold and wrapped around with strips of pale red velvet, and there was a large jewel that winked in the sunlight set into the pommel. But what amazed Colum more than anything else was that the entire length of the blade was etched and worked with the curling, twisting designs of the Tuatha De Danann.

Oisin held up the sword in both hands. The sunlight flowed down its length and caught in the design, bringing it to life, turning it into a bar of light. He twirled it once in the air, and then slid it into a plain black scabbard which was trimmed with silver.

'Let's sit down then, and I'll tell you my story.'

Chapter Four

The Legend

'I was hunting wild boar on the banks of the lakes of Killarney one fine spring morning with my father and the Knights of the Fianna when we first saw Niamh . . .' Oisin began . . .

Finn, chief of the Fianna, led the Knights of the Fianna down on to the sandy stretch of ground that bordered the lakeside. 'We'll rest here for a while,' he said, climbing down off his horse and handing the reins to his son, Oisin. 'That looks like a good spot over there,' he said, pointing off the track.

Oisin cantered his own horse over to a small group of trees and dismounted and tied both animals to a low branch. He blew gently in his own mount's ears and whispered softly to it, promising it some food and water soon, and then slowly made his way back to where his father and the other men were preparing their midday meal.

He stopped on a little rise and looked out over the still waters of the lake. They were flat and blue,

41

reflecting the cloudless sky and mirroring the tall, majestic mountains behind them.

He was about to turn away when there was a flash of light as something sparkled in the noonday sun on the surface of the water. He shaded his eyes with his hand and looked again. . . .

Yes! There was something there, moving across the water, something tall and white. . . . He squeezed his eyes shut for a moment and then looked again. It looked like a horse. But a horse riding on the top of the waves?

Magic! And magic usually meant trouble.

'Father! The lake; look at the lake.' He ran down to his father, pulling his sword free, pointing across the waves. His shouts brought the Knights of the Fianna to the water's edge, their weapons ready as they waited for the magical creature to come closer.

As it neared them, they could see that it was a tall, thin white horse, and it was ridden by a very beautiful young woman, whose hair was the colour of the sun and blew out behind her in the breeze like a cloak.

Finn stepped out from his men. The resemblance between him and his son was very strong; he was tall and well-built, and although

his red hair and beard were now flecked with grey, he was still the Champion of all Eriu.

The young woman drew up her magical horse a little distance away from Finn. As soon as the horse stopped moving, it slowly sank down into the water, and golden-brown sand settled over its silver-shod feet. She bowed gracefully to Finn and the Knights of the Fianna. 'I am Niamh,' she said softly, her voice gentle and almost musical, as if she were singing. 'I am the daughter of the King of Tir na nOg.'

Finn bowed deeply and his men put away their weapons. Tir na nOg was the Land of

Youth, and their weapons would be of no use against one of the fairy folk. 'I am Finn,' he said proudly, 'and this is my son, Oisin. . . .' He nodded towards the young man standing just behind him. 'What brings one of the fairy folk to Eriu?' he asked.

Niamh smiled strangely and, although she was talking to Finn, her eyes never left Oisin's face. 'I know about your son, Finn.' She paused and her eyes flickered back to Finn's face, which was now troubled. 'He is the reason I have travelled across the seas to Eriu.'

Finn looked towards Oisin, and then turned back to the young woman. 'How do you know about my son?' he asked. 'What do you want of him?'

Niamh smiled. 'Tales of his kindness and honesty and honour have travelled even to the farthest islands of the Other-world. I have heard reports of his goodness everywhere, and so I have travelled to Eriu to ask him to come back to the Land of Youth with me to become my husband.' She turned to Oisin. 'Will you?' Her question hung on the still noonday air, and even the birds in the trees grew silent, almost as if they were waiting for an answer.

The young man looked from the beautiful

young woman to his father and then turned back to her again. She smiled again and raised her right hand slightly, and suddenly her face seemed to light up as if it had been touched with the sun and everything else faded, becoming dim and shadowed.

'You will become King of Tir na nOg,' she promised him, her voice a hissing, whispering echo as if it came down a long tunnel.

Finn stepped back and took Oisin to one side. 'If you go with her you will not return to Eriu,' he said softly. His voice echoed his worries.

'You may return to your homeland whenever you wish,' Niamh said to Oisin, although Finn had whispered and Niamh should have been too far away to hear.

Oisin looked at his father, but all he saw was a dim shape. Everything else had faded; the trees, the mountains, the men and their horses standing behind him had vanished into a deep and impenetrable night. Only Niamh remained visible, bright and shining silver and gold in the gloom. 'She is very beautiful,' Oisin said to his father.

'But she is not human,' Finn insisted. 'Oh, I know she looks human, but she comes from the race of the Tuatha De Dannan. She is old, far, far older than she looks.'

'She looks so young,' Oisin whispered dreamily.

'I come from the Land of Youth,' Niamh said, still able to hear them even though they were now some little distance away. 'In my country there is no time. If you come there with me, you will not age, and you will not die.'

'And you will not return,' his father added. 'I will not – I cannot – allow you to leave.'

'You cannot stop him,' Niamh said, and then the white horse's hoof struck the water, the magical sound gathering into a solid wind that crashed into Finn and his warriors like a blow. They staggered back and some fell to the ground, while all around them, the leaves on the trees and bushes fell from their branches with the sound. Only Oisin had remained standing.

He moved away from his father and walked down to the water's edge. He stood by the head of the strange white horse and looked up into the young woman's bright green eyes. She leaned over and ran her fingers through his bright red hair. 'I love you, Oisin,' she said simply, and even though everything was strange, and Oisin felt as if he were dreaming, he sensed that the woman meant what she said.

'But you've never met me,' he said in surprise. 'How can you love me?'

'You are a good man, Oisin; kind, generous, honest and loyal. I love you for that. Come with me,' she pleaded.

'Can I refuse?' he asked, but Niamh merely smiled and said nothing.

Oisin looked over his shoulder to where he knew his father and the Knights of the Fianna should be, but all he saw were confused shadows. He turned back to Niamh and looked up into her eyes. They were very beautiful, and as he looked they seemed to grow larger and larger, until he could see nothing else but them.

'Come with me, Oisin, son of Finn, come with me to the Land of the Ever Young.'

And Oisin took hold of the saddle horn and pulled himself up on to the horse's back, behind the princess. She smiled triumphantly at Finn and then she turned the horse and they galloped back across the sea into the west.

Oisin did not look back . . .

'When I woke up, I was here.' Oisin finished simply.

'She enchanted you,' Colum said in a terrified whispcr, looking around almost as if he expected the fairy woman to appear suddenly.

The warrior nodded. 'I know.'

'But . . . but why didn't you try to leave?'

'I was deep under the enchantment at first,' Oisin said slowly, 'and then later, well . . .' he shrugged '. . . well, there was nothing to return for. My life, my family is here. This is my home now!'

Chapter Five

Oisin's Daughter

'This is my home now,' Oisin said slowly, turning the long sword around and around in his hand.

'But have you never wanted to go back?' Colum asked, when Oisin said nothing else.

'Sometimes,' Oisin admitted, staring into the waters of the little pool, 'but never seriously.' He looked at Colum. 'But there's never been a reason for me to return – not until now,' he added. He looked at the sword. 'I think it's time for me to pay a visit to my father,' he said.

'But, Oisin . . .' Colum began.

'And I'd better take you home; your parents will have become concerned about you.'

The boy nodded and was about to say something, when a young girl of about his own age came down the forest track, leading a snow-white unicorn. She stopped when she saw them, and the animal immediately took flight on its spindly legs.

Oisin looked up at the sound and he smiled as he stood up and held out a hand. The girl came

forward slowly, looking shyly from the boy to the man. 'This is Plure,' Oisin said, 'my daughter.'

Colum bowed to her, the stiff formal bow from a prince to a princess. He looked closely at the girl. It was more than a little frightening how like her mother she was. She had the same small triangular face, the same bright green eyes, and the same long butter-coloured hair. There seemed to be very little of her father in her, except perhaps that her hands were big, and her fingers short and stubby, like Oisin's. She was wearing a simple gown of green and silver, which had been made from some strange material, that shifted and billowed around her as she moved, and there were two plain golden torcs wrapped around her wrists.

'This is Colum,' Oisin said to the girl. 'He comes from my own land.'

The girl looked directly at Colum, but she looked at him as if he were some sort of strange animal, a curiosity, something she had never seen before. She then leaned in close to her father and whispered loudly enough for Colum to hear, 'Is he a "human", Father?'

Oisin laughed and ran his broad hands through his daughter's shining hair. 'Of course he's a human and, before you say anything about humans, remember, I'm a human too.'

But Plure didn't look too sure about that. She shook her head. 'You've lived here for so long now, Father, you've become one of us.'

Oisin saw Colum's puzzled look. 'When Plure says "us",' he said, 'she means the People of the Goddess, the Tuatha De Danann.'

'Yes, the finest people on this world,' Plure said, speaking to Colum for the first time. Her eyes were hard and held the same frightening power as her mother's, and Colum had no doubts but that she knew some magic.

The boy glanced at Oisin, and then he looked

back to the girl. 'Of course they are,' he said, 'they made the land of Erin what it is today.'

'Oh.' Plure looked disappointed, almost as if she had expected the boy to argue with her. 'Why have you come here?' she asked.

He shrugged. 'I didn't exactly come here; I was brought here by a strange white horse. . . .'

Plure nodded and smiled, showing her small white teeth. 'That would be Bainte; he does that sometimes. But he usually brings people here for a reason. . . .' She looked closely at the boy. 'I wonder why he brought you here?' She paused and then added proudly, 'He brought my father here also.'

Oisin grinned as he remembered. 'Aye, Niamh and I rode here on the same animal.' He picked up his sword, and rubbed a piece of clay from the end of the scabbard where it had been resting on the ground. 'I'll just put this away,' he said, and turned back towards his forge.

The boy and the girl stood looking shyly at each other for a few moments. Plure thought he was the ugliest creature she had ever seen, with his broad flat face and its red dots, his small nose and round chin. His eyes, although they were grey, were not the bright sharp colour of the fairy folk, but rather a deeper, muddier colour. Also, his arms were too short and his legs too fat, she decided. When he spoke, his voice was rough and harsh, unlike the musical speech of her own race.

'This island is very lovely,' Colum said. 'I've never seen so many beautiful plants and strange animals.'

'Your world must be very plain and ugly,' Plure said.

Colum shook his head. 'No, I don't think so, it's just different. You might like it,' he added.

The young girl shook her head, her long hair whispering loudly. 'No, I don't think so.' She looked around at the tall trees in the distance and the small sparkling lake. 'I'm sure you will come to love Tir na nOg, and forget the ugliness of your own world.'

Colum shook his head. 'No, I don't think so, I don't think I'll be here long enough; your father said something about taking me home. . . .' He stopped when he saw the strange look that came into the girl's eyes. 'What's the matter?'

'Did you say my father is going to take you home?'

Colum nodded. 'Yes. . . .'

'But that means he will have to leave Tir na

53

nOg,' Plure said in a sort of breathless amazement.

Colum frowned, puzzled at the girl's strange behaviour. 'I think he also said something about visiting Erin again.'

'But he can't. . . .' Plure began.

'I can't do what?' Oisin asked, coming out of his forge and walking across the grass towards them.

'You can't leave here,' Plure said, almost angrily.

'I wouldn't leave you, little one,' Oisin said, stooping down, 'but I think I will return to my own land for a few days. I want to escort Colum home, and then I can visit my family and some old friends. I'll be gone for two days, three at the most. You won't even miss me,' he added with a smile.

'But you can't leave here,' Plure said, her voice no more than a whisper, her green eyes wide and staring, 'not even for a single day!'

'Why not?' Oisin asked, with a laugh.

'Because . . . because you just can't!' Plure suddenly shouted. She glared at Colum. 'This is all your fault; why did you have to come here!' And then she turned around and ran down the track, her green and silver gown floating out behind her like a cloud.

Oisin stared after her in amazement. He had never seen his daughter like that before; indeed, he

54

had never heard her shout before either. Plure was a strange, almost secretive girl. She was so like her mother it was uncanny and, because the magic of the De Danann race was passed down from mother to daughter, Plure was already a fine sorceress – and that frightened her father a little. Oisin, even though he had lived on the magical isle for so many years now, still had the warrior's fear and loathing of magic and sorcery. He looked at Colum and then shrugged. 'Something's frightened her . . . probably you. Except for me, she's never seen another human person before; she's more used to the De Danann folk and their strange servants and the magical animals that roam these forests.'

Colum nodded doubtfully. 'But maybe she's right,' he said, 'maybe you shouldn't come back to Erin with me. Just give me a horse, and point me in the right direction.'

The tall warrior shook his head. 'No, I'm afraid that is impossible. Someone will have to take you back to Eriu, because you could not find it yourself.' He straightened up. 'And the only person who can take you back to Eriu is me.'

'But why. . . ?'

Oisin shrugged. 'Bainte may bring many

people from the real world into this fairy world, but he never takes anyone back. I'm afraid only I have the strength and power to make him do that, and only I know the route through the Shadowland that lies between your world and the fairy realm. Anyway,' he added, 'I want to give that sword to my father.'

'But Oisin . . .' Colum said.

The warrior raised his hand. 'No more; I will hear no more about it. I'm taking you home myself – and that is that!'

Niamh was waiting for Oisin and Colum when they returned to the tall tower. Her face seemed sharper than usual and her eyes were hard. She looked from the boy to her husband. 'Plure tells me you are going back to Eriu,' she said quickly, before Oisin could say anything. Colum found that her voice had lost some of its musical sweetness, and it was now harsh and sharp, like a harp played just a little out of tune.

The warrior nodded. 'Aye, I'll take Colum home, and I'll visit my people.'

'That might not be wise,' Niamh said, looking quickly from Oisin to Colum.

'Why not? Surely a brief visit can do no harm, and I'll be back in a day or two.'

'You have been away from Eriu for . . . for a long time now,' Niamh said slowly. 'There will have been changes.'

'How long have I been here?' Oisin asked.

'Longer than you think,' Niamh said, and Colum thought her voice sounded almost sad.

But Oisin just nodded. 'Well, I think it's time I returned home.'

'Are you not happy here?' she asked, reaching out her hand to touch Oisin's cheek.

'Of course I am,' Oisin said quickly. 'You are here and Plure is here; this is my home.'

'Then why do you suddenly want to return to Eriu after all this time?'

The man shrugged. 'I don't know.' He glanced down at Colum. 'The boy brings back memories of Eriu. Can you not smell the perfume of the heather and gorse, and the wild salt smell of the seas and the tang of the turf smoke that clings to him?'

Colum sniffed his sleeve, but he could smell nothing, and then he saw Niamh's cold, cold eyes turn and fix on him and he felt his breath catch in his throat. And he realized that this woman hated him. Not because he was human – but because he was taking her husband away from her.

'In all the years I've lived here, I've smelt nothing but the sweet scents of Tir na nOg, the gentle smells, the delicate odours, like the smells one experiences in a dream. The boy brings with him the harsh, raw smells of the real world.' He stopped, and then added simply, 'And it makes me homesick.'

Niamh stared at her husband for a few moments without saying anything, and then she nodded. 'Perhaps it would be as well for you to return.' She nodded again. 'I've only used my magic on you once, Oisin, son of Finn, and that was when I brought you here. But I loved you, you see, and because I still love you very deeply, I won't try and keep you here. But I could,' she added, glancing at Colum, 'I could make you stay.'

'I know you could,' Oisin smiled, 'but I don't think you would want that.'

Niamh shook her head. 'No, you must only stay here because you love Plure and me, not for any other reason.'

'And that is why I will return here,' Oisin said, 'because I love you both.'

The fairy woman nodded. 'I know. Return to the land of Eriu then, but remember, this will be the only time you will be able to do so – you have spent too long in the magic lands. And as for the changes you will find when you return home, well . . .' Niamh Golden Hair shot a glance at Colum as if warning him to say nothing, 'well. . . .' She kissed her husband quickly on the cheek and then she turned away.

Oisin stared at her with a puzzled frown on his face. Something was not quite right. First Plure and now Niamh asking him not to return home . . . but he was only going home for a few days, and then he would return to Tir na nOg and his family. He shook his head. Time would reveal all. He smiled down at Colum. 'Let's get you some supper and find a bed for you. Tomorrow we ride for Eriu!'

Chapter Six

Setting Out

'Why don't you make him stay?' Plure asked her mother, as they hurried down a long tree-lined track that led to the shore. 'You could make him stay if you wanted to.'

Niamh Golden-Hair nodded seriously. 'Yes, I could enchant him, and make him stay – so could you, if you really wanted to – but it wouldn't be right, would it?' She looked down into her daughter's wide eyes.

'And will it be right if he goes away and never returns?' Plure demanded angrily.

'We cannot keep him against his will,' Niamh said. 'He has been happy up to now, but this boy has brought back memories of his own land and he wants to return home for a visit. If I stop him from going, he will no longer be my husband and your father, Plure, he will have become a slave, a servant – and you don't want that do you?'

'You could stop Bainte from carrying him across the water,' the young girl suggested.

Niamh laughed. 'I'm not sure I could. Bainte is the Guardian of this Isle; everything he does is for Tir na nOg's protection. I cannot make him do anything against his will.' She paused, as a sudden thought struck her. 'And Bainte did bring the boy here, and now Oisin wants to go back with him.' There was a note of excitement in her voice. 'There must be some connection – there has to be; Bainte never does anything without a reason.'

'But what reason would he have for sending my father away?' Plure almost shouted. She was white-faced with anger and if she had been human she would have cried. But Plure was only half-human, and she could not cry.

'I don't know,' Niamh said softly, 'I really don't know.'

Plure was about to speak again, when she looked up and noticed how pale and drawn her mother's face was, and that there were shadows under her eyes. And the girl suddenly realized that her mother feared Oisin's leaving as much as she did. Did she also fear that he would not come back?

The sunrise turned the water into a mirror of pink and gold and sent long shadows dancing across the broad sandy beach. There was a gentle breeze blowing in off the sea, and Colum breathed in deeply, smelling the strange odours of herbs and spices it carried. Every breath he took, every sound he heard, every sight he saw reminded him that he was no longer in Erin, but in a fairy place – Tir na nOg.

And although when he was younger, all he had ever wanted to do was to visit one of the Secret Places of the Tuatha De Danann, now that he was here, he wanted nothing more than to leave it.

Colum turned away from the sea and looked back up the beach. Besides himself there were only three other people on it – Oisin, Niamh Golden-Hair and Plure. They were all dressed in their finest clothes, but then, perhaps the De Danann folk always wore the finest clothes. Niamh and Plure were both wearing long shimmering gowns of strange, metallic-looking cloth that had curious twisting patterns running down along the hems and round the collars. The colours were rich and bright and almost harsh on the soft morning air.

Oisin was dressed as a warrior of Erin; a simple woollen tunic, belted around the middle, and with leather sandals on his feet with thongs that wrapped around his legs almost up to the knee. There was a thick-bladed knife stuck into his belt, and the sword he had made for his father had been wrapped in cloth and was now strapped across his back. He also had a thick travelling cloak thrown across his arm — although the morning wasn't cold.

Colum was just beginning to wonder what he was supposed to do, when Oisin kissed his wife and daughter and then strode down the beach to the water's edge to stand beside him. The warrior stared out across the sea, and then he glanced sideways at the boy and smiled. 'We're going home, eh?'

Colum nodded, and then he too smiled at a sudden thought.

'What's so funny?' Oisin asked.

Colum grinned. 'Oh, I've just realized I'm going to ride back to Erin with a legend.'

Oisin laughed. 'Aye, that will be something to tell your friends about, eh?'

'But where's the horse?' the boy asked.

'Bainte?' Oisin asked, then nodded. He suddenly put two fingers into his mouth and gave a shrill high-pitched whistle that seemed to shatter the morning air. Birds rose wheeling up into the sky in the trees beyond the beach, screaming and cawing with the disturbance. Some darted down to the beach to investigate, and Colum took a step nearer the warrior when he realized just what they were. Because, although they could fly, they weren't birds. Some of them looked like bats – giant bats, bats as big as horses and with wings that must have been twice Oisin's height. They had long thin beaks and cold dead eyes. The bat-creatures swooped down, and then darted away again, but they came so close that the boy smelt their musty, musky scent and felt his eyes begin to water.

Oisin placed his arm protectively around Colum's shoulder. 'Oh, you needn't worry, they only eat plants and leaves, they have no taste for meat. Well, not the day-time birds anyway, the night-birds are a different matter. They help guard the island.' He waved one away, and it automatically snapped its long, long jaws at him, and Colum had a glimpse of hundreds of tiny pointed teeth.

'But I thought nothing evil lived on this land?' he said, looking at the bird-creatures.

Oisin tilted his head to one side, considering. 'This is the Land of No Time; creatures that have died out in our world still live here. And as

for evil, well, nothing deliberately evil lives
here, but there are still some dangerous beasts.'

'But why don't you kill them then?' Colum
asked.

'The De Danann folk do not believe in killing
animals. They believe every living thing has a
soul, and when it dies that soul passes on and is
reborn again in another shape and form.'

'Every living thing?'

Oisin nodded. 'Every living thing; trees,
flowers, bushes, weeds, fish, birds, beasts —
everything. . . .' The warrior stopped as something white moved through the trees and then

came clattering on to the rocks. It was Bainte. Blue-white sparks struck from his hooves and then he was down on to the soft sand, where he stopped beside Niamh and Plure.

'Will Oisin come back to us?' Niamh asked, and the horse whickered. 'Why did you bring the boy here? Why are you taking my husband away?' She asked the questions hurriedly, and the white horse whickered and whinnied softly to her, and then bowed his thin head and trotted up to Oisin and Colum.

'This is Bainte,' Oisin said in a whisper, running his broad hand down the horse's slender head. The cat-like eyes closed and Bainte twisted his head with pleasure. 'This is the White Horse of legend, a relative of Pegasus and his clan, the flying horses of the east.' He picked a leaf from the silken mane. 'The winged horses have all gone now and this is the last of the race – but luckily they are long-lived. Bainte came from the Shining City of Murias with the Tuatha De Danann when they first came to Eriu – and you know how long ago that was.'

Colum looked at the creature in awe. That would make Bainte . . . well, he wasn't exactly sure just how old it would make the horse, but thousands of years certainly, if not tens of thousands of years.

Niamh came down the beach with Plure, and they stood together before Oisin and Colum. 'You're going?' Niamh said very softly.

'You know I have to.'

'I know,' Niamh said almost sadly. 'Come back to us,' she said.

'Come back soon,' Plure added in a whisper.

'I will.' Oisin said. He stood, holding Niamh's and Plure's hands in his, while he looked lovingly at them both, and Colum, standing to one side, saw the tears sparkling in the warrior's eyes.

Finally Niamh let his hand fall. 'Go now, so that you can return all the sooner.'

Oisin nodded and turned away. He reached down and easily lifted the large saddle that had been waiting on the beach for the horse and then gently placed it over Bainte's slender back. The horse's head turned and he seemed to be watching him carefully.

The saddle itself was beautiful, the finest piece of leather-work Colum had ever seen — finer than any of his father's. It was high at both ends, making it look almost like a seat, and from end to end it had been carved and cut with hundreds of tiny figures, animals and men, faces and flowers, shapes and signs, figures and fancies that looked almost like the Ogham script of the Druids, but not quite. The leather-work was marvellously detailed, and the boy wondered how long it had taken to cut and shape the different coloured leathers and felts.

Oisin pulled the strap that went under the horse's belly tight – but not too tight – and then adjusted the reins. But the reins were really only something to hold on to, because there was no bit in the animal's mouth. If Bainte didn't want to go somewhere – he just wouldn't go.

The warrior then turned to his wife. 'Well. . . .' he began, and then he seemed to forget what he was about to say.

'Well. . . .' she said, and smiled.

Oisin smiled too and then he swept his wife up into his arms and held her tight. 'I won't be long,' he said. 'I'll be gone two days – three – at the most, and then I'll come back to you.'

'Promise?' she asked.

'Promise,' he said. He then knelt in the sand and gathered his daughter into his arms. 'I love you,' he said, his breath tickling her ear.

'I love you too,' she said very, very softly.

Oisin stood up and sighed. 'I had best be off. . . .' he said slowly, almost reluctant to leave now that the moment had arrived.

'There is one thing, Oisin,' Niamh said,

pointing to the horse. 'When you reach Eriu, you must not let go of Bainte.'

Oisin frowned. 'I don't understand.'

'You have been too long in this place,' Niamh said. 'You have absorbed a part of it – you might say this place is in you. We are a magical people, Oisin, but you are only *almost* magical and, at the moment, you belong to neither your own world nor this fairy place. But Bainte is a part of this world, and if you hold on to him, then this magical place still has some hold over you.'

'Don't let go, Father,' Plure said softly. Her face was very pale and her eyes looked almost too bright and sparkling.

Oisin knelt down in the damp sand again and kissed his daughter. 'I won't. I'll bring you back a surprise from Eriu,' he said with a wink.

'Remember, don't let go of the horse; in fact it would be better if you didn't get off Bainte at all,' Niamh said.

Oisin swung up on to Bainte's slender back and then reached down for Colum's hand. 'I promise,' he said.

Colum turned to Niamh and Plure and bowed deeply. 'My Lady, I thank you for your hospitality. . . .'

Niamh smiled and inclined her head slightly.

The boy looked at Plure, opened his mouth to say something but the look in her eyes made him close it again. 'Good-bye,' he said simply. He turned to look up at the warrior, and Oisin reached down and pulled the boy up behind him.

'Come back soon,' Plure said, as Bainte turned around and began to splash out through the surf into the deeper water.

'Come back to us,' Niamh whispered, as the horse began to trot, and water splashed up on either side. She then saw the animal begin to rise up out of the water, and knew that the two riders were feeling the tingle of magic as it made its way through their bodies. Now Bainte was trotting across the top of the waves and, even with two riders on his back, not even breaking the surface.

'Why did you let them go, Mother?' Plure asked as they watched the magical horse splash out through the waves, with its two riders.

'Because Bainte advised me to let him go,' Niamh said. She knelt in the sand and held her daughter close. 'Bainte brought Colum here for a reason; he brought him here to remind Oisin of his homeland, and I suppose to give him an excuse to go home.'

'But why?'

'Because Bainte says that your father has become more and more dissatisfied with life here in Tir na nOg over the past few years. It is one of the reasons for his many hobbies. Bainte says that if we didn't give Oisin the chance to go home now, we might have woken up one morning and found him gone anyway. This way, Oisin knows he can return here to us; if he ran away, he would never return.'

'But will he return?' Plure demanded. 'Surely your magic can tell you that?'

'I'm afraid it cannot. My magic is not as strong now as it once was, and I cannot see across the huge distance that separates Tir na nOg from Eriu.'

'So we don't know if he will return?' Plure asked, frightened now.

Her mother could only shake her head. 'We don't know.'

Chapter Seven

The Shadowland

'How long did it take you to reach Tir na nOg?'
Oisin asked as they galloped out across the
waves.

Colum held on tightly to Oisin's belt and
pressed his face against the warrior's broad back,
out of the whipping wind. He knew now why
Oisin had brought a cloak – that breeze was cold!
'I don't know,' he shouted. 'I set out at night, but I
fell asleep, and when I awoke, the sun was coming
up. I think it might have been just one night, but
somehow it felt longer.'

He felt Oisin nod. 'When I came here with
Niamh all those years ago, our journey lasted three
days, and we spent a further three days on an
island where I fought a terrible Fomorian demon.'

'I don't remember passing any islands on my
way here,' Colum said.

'Well, you might have slept through the whole
journey, but there are many pathways to the Land
of Youth,' Oisin said. 'You were lucky you didn't

fall prey to one of the many dangers that surround the isle.'

'What sort of dangers?' Colum asked.

Oisin suddenly pointed off to one side. 'That sort!' he shouted.

Colum looked away to the right, and at the same time Bainte seemed to slow down, so the boy could see clearly. He found he was looking at an island – a small rocky island that was completely surrounded by a golden wall. The island was further divided in two by a silver wall, and there were scores of small black and white bundles moving about on either side of the wall, with black to the left hand side and white bundles on the right. Colum squinted through the spray, trying to identify the strange shapes. 'They're sheep,' he said in astonishment.

Oisin nodded. 'Aye, and there's the shepherd.'

Colum almost let go of Oisin with fright as a huge figure suddenly reared up on the island. It was man-shaped, but it was not a man. It was huge, easily standing as tall as the tower on Tir na nOg. It was hard to make out whether the figure was male or female because it was covered in long filthy black hair, and only its two burning eyes were visible as they glared across at the white horse with its two riders. It raised a huge hand that seemed to have far too many fingers and shook a club at them that was taller than a tree, and then it stooped down, picked up something and flung it at the riders. The man and boy ducked as a monstrous boulder shot through the air directly towards them – but then Bainte put on a spurt of speed and the huge rock crashed into the sea behind them, drenching them.

Two more rocks followed, but they were now out of range and all the giant could do was bellow in rage and shake its huge club in the air.

'What was that?' Colum asked, his voice trembling with fright.

'I don't know,' Oisin said, 'all Niamh would tell me was that it was called the Shepherd. The sheep you saw are the travellers it has captured as they rode or sailed across this sea. It changes them into animal forms so they can never escape.'

'But I've never heard of an island like that off Erin's coasts,' Colum protested.

'Ah, but we're not off Eriu's coasts now,' the warrior insisted. 'This is the Shadowland, this is the world that lies between your world and the realm of Tir na nOg. Magic is still strong here, and you will see many strange and wonderful sights. Ah! I remember these from the last time,' the warrior suddenly said.

He pointed again, and the boy saw a young snow-white deer, which was being chased by a large red-eyed, red-eared dog which had a scorpion's stinger instead of a tail. 'The creature never catches the deer,' Oisin said, and then he turned to the other side and added, 'nor does the warrior catch the maiden.'

Colum turned around and saw a young woman riding a deep chestnut-coloured horse being chased by a strange-looking warrior riding a snow-white mount, that looked perhaps too much like a dog to be truly called a horse. The warrior, too, did not seem to be truly human; his skin was a stark white colour and his eyes were a deep, almost purple red. Colum also noticed that he was waving a long-handled golden sword. Every so often the maiden would glance over her shoulder and then her mouth would open as if she were screaming, but neither the man nor boy heard any sound.

Oisin then clapped his heels to Bainte's side and the horse, which had slowed down, picked up speed again. Soon they rode into a group of small islands. 'We must take great care now,' Oisin said. 'These islands are like a great key, they are laid out in a pattern and we must sight each of them in a certain order so that we may return to Eriu. In their way, they are all dangerous, and each one has the power to trap us.'

'But I thought Bainte's magic would protect us,' Colum said, looking around fearfully at the islands that were rising up out of the sea.

'In part, yes, but a lot of his magic – his power – is spent in just riding the waves and, because you are human, and there is still a lot of the human world about me, that will only serve to weaken his magic further.'

'What do we do?' Colum asked.

Oisin looked back over his shoulder and smiled. 'We take great care,' he said.

They had now ridden into the islands, and as Colum looked around, he found that each one seemed to be even more wondrous than the last. They passed one that was swarming with birds – thousands upon thousands of birds, some small and dark, others brightly coloured. The noise was incredible; each bird seemed to be singing, whistling, cackling, cawing, screaming, shouting, mewling and chirruping at the same time. They rose above the island in a thick dark cloud and had no sooner settled down on the branches of the ancient-looking trees and bushes, than another flock rose up into the air.

A few spotted the white horse and flew out to investigate, but Bainte laid his long ears back and picked up speed, almost as if he were afraid of the creatures.

The next island had a tree growing on it – a single huge tree. Colum at first thought it was a whole forest, but as Bainte drew closer, he discovered it was indeed just one tree – an apple tree. And it was in fruit. Huge red and gold apples hung down from every branch, some of them bending so low as to touch the water, and as the white horse galloped closer, Colum took a tighter hold on Oisin's belt and began to lean across. . . .

'Don't!' Oisin suddenly shouted and, at the same time, Bainte lurched to one side, away from the trees.

'I only wanted an apple,' Colum said, both startled and frightened by Oisin's shout.

'Look back,' Oisin said, and Colum turned around in the high saddle and looked back over his shoulder. He saw the huge ripe apple he had been going to reach for – and then he saw the slimy black tentacle that came up from beneath the water and wrapped itself around the fruit. 'Don't touch anything,' Oisin ordered him. 'Everything in this Shadowland has its guardian.'

Colum swallowed hard and nodded. He felt

himself shuddering at the thought of that black snake-like tentacle wrapping itself around him.

There were other islands, but the white horse didn't come too close to these. The boy saw giant ants on one, terrible demon horses on another, huge snakes slithered and fought with long-bodied lizards on another. Each island seemed more frightening and dangerous than the last.

The white horse galloped on into the morning and then Colum felt a tingle run through his body – like that he had felt when Bainte was using his magic to rise up out of the water. He looked down – but the horse was still galloping across the surface of the waves. And then he looked down again. Beneath the horse's hooves, the water was changing in colour from a sparkling blueness to a pale milky colour. Colum looked around, and found the white stain was spreading. Soon the entire sea was milk-white.

'Close your eyes,' Oisin commanded. 'If you stare too long at this whiteness, it can rob you of your sight. I'll tell you when you can open them again.'

Colum squeezed his eyes shut – and already they were watering and felt gritty – and pressed

his head against Oisin's back. He was glad now he had slept on the ride over to Tir na nOg; otherwise he would surely be dead or at the very least blind by now.

After a while, he felt the same almost painful pins-and-needles in his arms and legs, and he guessed that they must be passing out of the magical white sea, and almost at the same time, Oisin said, 'You can open your eyes now; it's safe.'

Colum sighed and blinked open his eyes, and then he glanced down – and shouted aloud with fright. There was no water below them, they were riding through the air!

'Ois . . . Ois . . . Oisin,' he stuttered.

The warrior glanced over his shoulder and smiled encouragingly. 'Don't worry,' he said, 'this is the Sea of Glass. The water is perfectly clear, but there is still water there. Look!' He pointed and Colum looked down into the crystal clear water and saw the wreck of a strange ship half-buried in the ground.

'But why can't we see the water?' Colum asked.

'I asked Niamh the same question,' Oisin said. 'She told me then that the water was so pure and so clean that there were no impurities in it to reflect the light.'

Colum shook his head. 'I'm not sure I understand.'

'I'm not sure I do either,' Oisin said, 'but I think it's something like this. We see blue water because it reflects the blue of the sky, and we see grey sea when the sky is clouded over. But don't forget, water is colourless and what we are seeing is the colour of the sky reflecting off the tiny pieces of dirt and sand in the water. However, this water is clean and pure. . . .'

'. . . And there is nothing in it to reflect the light,' Colum finished.

Oisin nodded. 'Just so.'

Colum stared down at the sea-bed, fascinated. It was difficult to believe that he wasn't flying – this must be very like what the birds see when they soared and wheeled over the land. He saw other wrecks now, the remains of a huge fleet that must have sunk in these waters, and then further on he saw the regular shapes of buildings. Bainte changed direction slightly, and his new route led directly over the first of these. It was a huge square shape, surrounding a series of smaller squares, and it took the boy a few moments to realize that he was looking down on a walled house with a courtyard and that the circular shape in the centre must have been a fountain.

Soon they were riding above the remains of a city – and what must have been a huge city too. Colum had never seen anything like it, nor had Oisin for that matter, although Niamh had told him tales of the Four Cities of the Tuatha De Danann that were each supposed to spread over an entire country.

'What happened here?' Colum asked, his voice dropping to a whisper.

'The gods destroyed it,' Oisin said. 'It was once a great and powerful land, stretching from one side of the broad Western Ocean to the next. However, its people became too proud and its magicians grew powerful, and soon they were proclaiming themselves to be even greater than the gods. But the gods heard them and so, in three days and three nights, the seas rose up and the land sank beneath the waves.'

'Did anyone escape?'

Oisin nodded. 'A few did, fleeing before the storm in vessels that are not unlike the curragh-boats in Eriu. They settled in the lands that bordered the Western Ocean. Some of them even came to Eriu, where they found and fought the Tuatha De Danann for the land.'

'And they won?' the boy asked.

'They won. You see, even though the De

Danann possessed powerful magic, they were an old people and a tired race, and had no wish to fight, and the new invaders brought with them a terrible weapon – iron. And the fairy folk cannot abide iron. That is one of the reasons they left for the Secret Places. Our people are descendants of the invaders from the Sunken Lands.' Oisin looked over his shoulder and smiled again. 'Well, perhaps not your folk nor mine, not with our red hair and light skin. The invaders were dark-haired, dark-eyed, pale-skinned folk.'

'But what about our ancestors; the red-haired, green and grey-eyed peoples?' Colum asked, interested now.

Oisin shrugged. 'I'm not sure where they came from, but my father always said they came across from the lands from the east. He had travelled there, and had met many others with similarly coloured hair, skin and eyes.'

Colum nodded. 'That's what one of my teachers told me.'

They had ridden beyond the sunken city and now the sea had once more changed back to its normal blue colour, and they were approaching another island. They could see this one from a great distance because there was a single tall silver pillar set dead centre on it, and rising up into the clouds. As they approached they saw that both the island and the pillar were huge. It was impossible to say how tall or how broad the pillar was, but it took Bainte several minutes to gallop past it, and Colum craned his neck back so far as he looked up that he almost fell off the horse. But the pillar just went up and up and up. . . .

The column seemed to be carved from solid silver, and there were many thousands of tiny pictures etched into its long sides. Some showed ships at sea, and others showed a huge city, just like the one they had ridden over, while still more showed terrible monsters stalking through the streets, or fighting strange armies armed with curious weapons, and then the last set of pictures showed a large fleet of ships setting sail, while behind them more of the monstrous creatures chased them in even stranger craft.

Colum wondered what had happened to the people shown in the pictures and, more importantly, what had happened to the hideous creatures that had been chasing them. And he also wondered who had made the incredible tower. He asked Oisin, but the warrior shook his head.

'I don't know. No one, not even the Tuatha De Danann know that. However, the monsters shown on the side of the tower are the ancestors of the Fomorians, the demons who fought the People of the Goddess when they first came to the land of Eriu. I fought one of them on my way to Tir na nOg with Niamh. Ah, now that was a battle,' Oisin said with a grin. 'It lasted three days and three nights, but in the end I killed him. And look, there's the very isle!'

Colum looked and saw a small rocky island lying off to one side. It looked very normal, in fact it looked so normal that Colum looked again, just in case he was missing something.

'There used to be a fort there,' Oisin pointed to a tumbled pile of stones. 'The demon had taken one of the De Danann folk prisoner and was holding her in there. She was related to Niamh somehow, I'm not sure how – but all the People of the Goddess are related to one another. Anyway, I fought him on that beach and killed him there.' Colum looked and saw a large stretch of the beach was burnt and blackened as if a huge fire had blazed there.

'Can we land, can I see?' Colum asked eagerly.

Oisin started to shake his head, and then he

shrugged. 'Yes, why not. Nothing lives on the island now, I don't think there can be any danger.' He smiled. 'I wouldn't mind the chance to stretch my legs.' He patted Bainte's head, and then pointed towards the island, without saying a word.

The horse immediately changed direction and headed for the island, but just as its feet struck the pebbled beach, both the man and boy felt the burning tingle of magic and the horse settled down into the water. He wouldn't go up on to the beach. Oisin climbed down and then reached for Colum, swinging him up on to his broad shoulders, and then he splashed through the shallows on to the beach.

He swung the boy down and pointed to the pile of large broken stones. 'The demon had his fort there, but when I killed him, it fell apart.'

Colum wandered down the beach to look at the ruins, while Oisin sat down on a large boulder, and began rubbing at his stiffened legs. It had been a long time since he had last ridden a horse for so long, and his muscles felt sore and tight.

Colum clambered over the stones, looking at the ruins. The stones were dirty, streaked with black marks and some of them even looked as if they had been melted by an intense heat. In a nook between the stones something sparkled in the sun and Colum reached for it . . . and then he hissed in surprise and pulled back his hand. He had grazed it on a rock and a long thin cut had opened along his little finger and the side of his hand. He shook his hand, annoyed with himself for not being more careful, and then he reached in again for the shining object. It was a piece of black stone, rough on one side, but smooth and polished like a mirror on the other, and it was this which had reflected the light. And while he examined it closely, a single drop of blood dripped from his cut and fell to the ground, where it was quickly absorbed into the blackened, scorched sands.

And the sands moved.

Chapter Eight

The Demon of Ice and Fire

A second drop of Colum's blood fell on to the sand, and then immediately vanished. And a single grain fell, and then another . . . and then the countless grains of sand moved again, shifting and rolling together, whispering, hissing, shushing together, until all the blackened, scorched grains had joined up . . . into a shape.

Colum held up the stone and allowed the sunlight to catch it. Bright, rainbow colours ran across its black polished surface like liquid. Behind the boy a shape rose up, sand cascading from it. . . .

Colum tilted the stone and looked into it . . . and found himself looking into the face of a demon!

His scream brought Oisin running, his sword in his hand. He scrambled down to the beach to find Colum facing a monster. He shouted, and the creature looked up and, while its attention was distracted, Colum darted away, and raced up to the warrior.

'Behind me,' Oisin shouted, 'get behind me.' He swung his sword around in both hands, while the monster lumbered up slowly, his four arms swinging loosely.

'What is it, what is it?' Colum shouted, looking properly at the creature for the first time.

'It's the Demon of the Isle, the Demon of Ice and Fire,' Oisin said slowly, 'but I thought I killed it. . . .'

The creature was hideous; it was rather like a serpent that had grown legs, but he had the beak and claws of a bird, and his eyes were that of a cat. It had four arms and a long scaled tail swished through the sands and rocks behind it.

'You killed me once,' the creature said, its voice hissing, its long forked tongue darting, 'but the boy's blood brought me back to life again, and human blood is life to me.' It laughed, the sound terrifying.

Colum looked at the cut on his hand; it was only a scrape, but the single drop of blood had been enough to bring the monster back to life.

'I killed you once,' Oisin said, tilting his sword, 'and I'll do it again.'

The demon laughed once more, and Colum shivered with the sound. 'No, I don't think so,' it said, and then it struck out at Oisin with one long curved talon. 'The last time I used my Fire Magic,' the demon growled, 'but now I think I should try the Ice Spells.' The warrior darted back as the creature struck again, and this time he managed to ward off the blow but as soon as Oisin's metal sword struck the demon's talon, there was a icy waft of cold air, and the weapon was immediately covered in thick, freezing ice. With a cry of pain Oisin dropped the sword and it was so cold it shattered into a hundred pieces on the stones. Icy patches formed on Oisin, and white frost coated his beard and hair, and sparkled on his woollen cloak. His skin turned blue with the cold and his breath plumed white and smoky on the air.

'I have you now!' the demon roared, and it reached out with all four arms.

Colum turned and raced down the beach, splashing into the water to where Bainte still stood patiently, watching the man and the demon without much interest. 'Help him, can't you, help him,' he shouted, but the horse just ignored the boy.

And then Colum remembered the sword

Oisin had made on Tir na nOg for his father. It was strapped to the horse. He grabbed the bundle and his fingers fumbled at the knots, pulling off covering after covering, until he finally reached the plain sheath. . . .

On the beach, Oisin was in trouble. He had managed to escape most of the demon blows because the creature was so slow and so clumsy. But its last blow had struck him and, although it hadn't hurt him, it had sent him crashing to the ground. He was now almost completely covered in a thick white frost, and his fingers were so numb he could barely move them, and he had no feeling in his legs and feet. He tried to stand up, but he slipped back on the icy, polished stones.

The monster lumbered up and stood over him. 'I am going to kill you, Oisin,' he roared, and raised his four arms, his talons spread.

Colum knew he was not going to reach Oisin in time; he was too far away. There was only one thing he could try. The boy pulled the sword free and then, holding it like a spear, took a deep breath, drew back his arm . . . and threw.

The demon's dagger-like claws dipped towards Oisin, and the warrior closed his eyes and breathed a silent prayer to his gods. . . .

The sword struck the monster in the back. There was a sudden explosion of sound and Oisin opened his eyes just in time to see the demon burst into flames, blue flames that burned without heat or sound. It sank to the ground, and its ice-magic spell faded from the warrior, and Oisin scrambled out of the way as the creature melted down into a blackened smoking pool on the beach – leaving the shining sword standing unmarked and unblemished in the centre.

Oisin said nothing but lifted up the sword and saluted Colum as a warrior. Together, they walked down the beach and Oisin climbed up on to Bainte's back, and then pulled the boy up behind him. They rode for the rest of the afternoon in silence, both of them thinking how close they had come to death.

It was late in the afternoon when Colum spotted something. 'What's that ahead?' he asked, pointing to a long thin black line that had appeared on the horizon.

Oisin looked up and then he gave a huge shout. He pressed his heels tightly against Bainte's side, and leaned over and whispered something in its twitching ears. The horse picked up speed and soon it was racing across the water. The line on the horizon quickly came nearer and clearer, and it became obvious that they were cliffs; tall black cliffs.

Colum sat bolt upright. There was something very familiar about those cliffs!

Quickly, very quickly they approached the land, and soon the tall black cliffs towered above their heads, and the noise of the waves dashing and pounding on the rocky beaches and against the base of the cliffs was deafening.

'The Cliffs of Moher,' Oisin shouted above the noise. The cliffs ran along part of Erin's western coast.

'Welcome home, Oisin,' Colum shouted. 'Welcome back to Erin.'

Chapter Nine

The Last of the Fianna

'I'm not sure where we are exactly,' Oisin said, as he urged Bainte up the stony beach towards a cleft in the cliffs.

Colum squirmed around in the saddle. 'What's that haze on the horizon?' he asked, pointing out to sea.

Oisin shaded his eyes with his hand and squinted out into the late morning air. 'An island,' he said slowly, 'it looks like an island.' He squeezed his eyes shut, opened them and then looked again. 'Maybe more than one island, I'm not sure.'

'They could be the Isles of Aran,' Colum said slowly.

Oisin nodded, and then smiled. 'Yes, indeed; so they could.' He took a deep breath, tasting the fresh salt air and feeling the sea spray on his face. This was what he remembered about Eriu! He remembered standing by the foot of the tall cliffs one summer's evening a long, long time ago, watching a storm out at sea and waiting for the waves he knew would soon come pounding in. He remembered just standing there, waiting for night to fall, getting wetter and wetter with the spray, and with the roaring of the sea against the cliffs getting louder and louder as the daysounds faded. He remembered it all so clearly. Oisin stretched his arms wide. 'It's good to be home,' he shouted, and his voice echoed off the tall, dark-stoned cliffs.

They rode up through a crack in the cliffs along a pathway that had obviously been made by goats some time in the past, although there was now grass and weeds growing across it, showing that it had not been used for a long time. Once at the top of the cliffs, Oisin gave Bainte his head, and the white horse began to gallop across the stony flatland. . . .

Oisin frowned.

'What's wrong?' Colum asked, seeing the strange look come into the warrior's eyes.

'The colours,' Oisin said.

'The colours?' the boy asked. 'What's wrong with the colours?'

Oisin frowned again, and drew Bainte to a slow walk. 'The colours are all so dull. Look!'

and his arm swept out in a half circle before him.

Colum looked around. Everything looked much as it should be. He saw an almost flat landscape, with the white rock beneath barely covered by a thin carpet of pale, hard grass. The rock was scored and broken, and long thin lines – like sword-cuts – sliced across it. Within these lines, richer, darker grass and brightly coloured flowers sprouted in abundance. There were a few stunted and twisted trees dotted here and there, and in the distance he could see the straight white line of a road.

'Look at the colours, look at the colours!' Oisin said again.

The boy looked again – and then he knew what Oisin meant. The colours did indeed seem dull when compared with the vivid, bright, almost harsh colours of Tir na nOg. Even the sky, which was a clear and cloudless blue, seemed just a little murky, and the sun looked more orange than bright gold.

'The colours were different in Tir na nOg,' he said slowly.

Oisin nodded sorrowfully. 'Even the air tasted different.'

The boy took a deep breath, but all he could

taste and smell was the rich salty smell of the sea and the fainter, sweeter smell of grass and flowers.

The warrior suddenly pointed. 'What's that?'

Colum followed the direction of his pointing finger and squinted into the distance. 'It's a road.' He pointed off to one side. 'Look, there's another.'

'There were no roads this far west when I left Eriu,' Oisin said, and Colum saw a strange expression flicker across his face; he wasn't sure what it was, but for a single moment, he had imagined it might be fear. 'Hang on,' the warrior shouted, and then he clapped his heels to Bainte's sides and the white horse took off at a gallop, seeming to skim across the rocky flatland, its gold-shod hooves barely touching the grass.

Oisin drove the horse on through the morning, hurrying ever eastwards. No normal horse would have been able to keep up the pace, but Bainte didn't even seem winded by the hard ride. They leaped rivers and streams, and once Oisin pulled Bainte to a halt and stared with a strange look in his eyes at a broad wooden bridge that spanned a tributary of the river Shannon. But the warrior seemed determined to avoid any humans, and whenever they saw the smoke from a cooking fire rising into the still morning air, he urged the white horse away from it. He kept to the woods, and stayed well clear of the roads, and he only spoke to Colum once, and that was when the boy had asked him where they were going.

'To Tara!' Tara was the home of the kings of Erin, and had been for generations. The simple palace was built on a rounded hill in the eastern part of the country, but even with the magical horse, Colum doubted if they would reach it in one day.

The day wore on and the sun rode slowly across the heavens, lengthening, then shortening their shadows until they were just simple pools of darkness beneath them, and then as the sun shifted into the afternoon, their shadows began to grow again.

Colum dozed part of the time; the gentle rocking motion of the horse lulling him to sleep. When he woke up, he would find himself in a different part of the country, either lush grasslands, thick, almost impenetrable forests or rolling hills. They stopped late in the afternoon, and the boy started awake to find the warrior staring at the ruins of an ancient fort on a hill in the distance. But Oisin pulled Bainte's head away before the boy could say anything and they continued galloping eastwards without saying a word.

Towards evening, when the sun had almost disappeared below the horizon behind them, and their shadows danced out long and thin ahead of them, they passed through a short rain shower. It brought Colum wide awake.

'Where are we?' he asked, with a shiver, although the shower was now behind them, and the sky overhead was streaked with pink and purple clouds. Already some of the night stars were beginning to twinkle.

'Nearly there,' Oisin said softly. 'We rode south and east for most of the day, so now we are to the south of Tara, in the mountains of Wicklow. We may stop here overnight, and continue on in the morning.'

Colum nodded. 'That's a good idea . . . look,' he said suddenly, 'the sea – and there are some people.' He stopped, and added, 'What are they doing?'

They had stopped on the brow of a hill and Oisin looked down into the field beneath at a small group of people clustered around a pile of boulders. He shook his head. 'I don't know.' He urged Bainte around and the white horse trotted down towards the group.

There were about twenty people in the centre of the field that sloped down towards the sea-shore. They were gathered around a pile of tumbled stones, and some of them were holding long tree trunks and looked as if they were trying to shift some of the stones. Everything stopped when the huge red-haired and bearded warrior riding the strange, thin white horse trotted through the long grass towards them. And in the silence that followed the cry of pain that came from the centre of the group was very clear.

Oisin frowned. Just what were these people doing? He looked at the group. They seemed normal enough, except that some of their clothes looked a little strange, especially the two men who stood a little to one side, and who were dressed in long brown robes of rough wool tied about the middle with a white cord. Their heads were bald in the centre, although there was still some hair left on their heads, and they wore strange crosses about their necks.

Someone moaned again, and then Colum slid down off Bainte's slender back and ran into the group, pushing people out of the way. 'Stand

102

back. I'm Prince Colum, and I want to know what's going on here. . . .' He stopped suddenly. He saw now what the men had been attempting to do. There was a pile of stones in the centre of the field, and some of these had fallen on an old man. The men had been attempting to lift the stones off the man before he was crushed.

One of the men in the brown robes stepped up. 'Prince Colum, where have you been? Everyone has been so worried, and there are search parties out everywhere. . . .'

Colum waved the questions aside. 'Can't you help him?' he asked, looking down at the trapped man.

The brown-robed priest shook his head. 'We've tried, but the stones are too heavy. He was crawling beneath a dolmen looking for treasure when the stones toppled and fell on him.'

Colum knelt down on the ground which had been churned to mud and peered in through the mass of boulders at the white-haired man. Amazingly, the man seemed to be largely unhurt, although when the stones had fallen he had been cut a little by flying pebbles. The boy stood up, shaking his head. Surely everyone knew that dolmens were dangerous, and besides, to tamper with them meant disturbing the ghost of the warrior who was buried beneath. A dolmen was a huge flat table of stone, resting on three upright stones, and marked the spot where some great warrior or hero was buried. Sometimes, people thought there was treasure buried there too, but when they went digging, they often found nothing, and more than once the stones had fallen on them. And that was what had happened here. Colum looked back at Oisin. 'Can you help?'

The warrior urged his horse forward, and the men quickly moved aside, some making the Sign of the Cross and others making the older signs of ancient gods. They could all sense the strangeness about this wild-looking man and his otherworld mount. He looked at the stone and then looked around at the men in amazement. 'But it's only a few stones, surely you can lift it?'

Some of the men laughed and shook their heads. 'Why, no single man could lift that great weight.'

'Any man – or boy – of the Fianna could lift those puny blocks without even trying,' he said proudly.

Someone nodded. 'Aye, one of the Fianna would be able to do it – if there were any left!'

Oisin glared at the man. 'What do you mean?' he demanded, but just then the stones shifted and the trapped man gave another piteous moan.

'Oisin, please help him,' Colum said.

The warrior nodded and was just about to dismount when Colum ran up to him. 'Remember Niamh's warning,' he said. 'You must not stand on the ground.'

Oisin nodded, and settled himself again in the saddle. He urged his horse right up against the pile of stones and leaned over and grabbed the first of them in his broad flat hands. He heaved. The stone grated and then tumbled through the air to land with a thump half-way across the field. More and more stones flew out of the pile, until just one stone remained, and this was the great table-like top of the dolmen which had fallen first. It was close to the ground, and Oisin had to lean far out of the saddle to grab it. His short stubby fingers took hold of the edge of the smooth stone, and then the muscles in his arms and on up into his neck strained as he heaved . . . and heaved . . . and heaved. . . .

Suddenly the stone gave a terrific crack and split in two. One half shot across the field . . . but the shock sent Oisin tumbling from the saddle!

Oisin cried out in rage and anger – but the shout turned to a croak when he hit the ground.

Colum raced to his side and caught his hand, but the hard-muscled, calloused hand the boy held began to twist and turn and shrivel up, the knuckle bones and joints grew larger and thick blue veins popped up on the back of the hand. The hand that had heaved away huge stones was now as frail as a bird's wing. The warrior's mane of red-hair and beard turned instantly white and most of it fell out, and his clear piercing green eyes dimmed and faded. Oisin's body too seemed to shrivel in on itself, and now the once-tall warrior was no bigger than the boy.

'Oisin!' Colum shouted, 'Oisin.' The boy saw the old man's shrivelled lips moving, and he bent his head close to Oisin's mouth to catch his words.

'The . . . the sword,' Oisin mumbled, 'take the sword. . . .'

Colum nodded. He was crying now, and his tears fell on to the old man's face. It was his fault – his fault Oisin had returned to Erin.

'Take the sword . . . and cast it into the sea,' the old man gasped.

'But it's special, it's magical, I can't just. . . .'

Oisin's face tightened in pain, and he closed his eyes briefly, before taking a laboured breath and

hurrying on. 'I know what's happened now. I . . . I should have guessed. You . . . you almost told . . . told me so many times.'

'Time was different in Tir na nOg; it passed much more slowly,' Colum said, sobbing bitterly.

'But I didn't realize just how much time. So much has happened now; so much has gone. And . . . and that's why you must take the sword . . . take the sword and cast it into the sea.' The old man's gnarled hands gripped Colum's tunic tightly. 'And you must call upon Manannan the Lord of the Sea and Fand, his wife. They will safeguard the sword. Take it,' Oisin said with a sigh, and then he lay back on the trampled grass.

Two of the brown-robed priests bustled up and spread a rough woollen blanket on the ground beside the withered old man. Then they carefully unbuckled his armour and lifted him on to it. Colum bent down and took up the sword in its plain black silver-trimmed scabbard. He watched as the priests carefully lifted up the blanket with the old man wrapped securely in it.

'Where are you taking him?' he asked, his voice trembling.

'We'll take him to Saint Patrick,' one of the priests said, and the boy nodded. He knew Oisin would be well looked after there, and when he reached Tara, he would make sure he received the best possible care and treatment.

He looked after the priests and for a moment he saw the wizened face, and he saw the thin lips move. . . .

'The sword. . . .'

Colum held the sword tightly in both hands and ran off towards the beach.

However, the beach was much further away than it seemed, and by the time he reached it, night had almost fallen. Colum stood on the shore, with the silver water foaming in around his feet, and for a single moment he hesitated. He looked at the sword. Surely it would be a great crime to destroy such a magnificent piece of work? It should be kept; it was the last of the magical weapons; a weapon fit for a king. The boy placed the scabbard on the sand and slowly drew out the shining length of metal, with its delicately beautiful workmanship.

It truly was a magical blade. And then the boy slid the sword back into its scabbard with a snap. He had seen what magic could do! He had seen it change a tall strong man into an ancient. He held the weapon above his head like a spear and then, facing the sea he called upon the old pagan gods to receive it.

'Manannan, Dark Lord of the Sea and Fand, Mistress of the Waves, receive this sword, the work of Oisin, the last of the Fianna.'

Then he threw it with all his might out over the dark waves.

And just before it hit the water a slender, silver-scaled arm shot out and a webbed hand caught it! Lightning flared in the sky overhead and for a single moment the sword blazed with light, and then the arm and sword disappeared.

'And that is how Oisin came back to the Land of Erin. I don't know what happened to Niamh or Plure or if they even knew that Oisin wouldn't be coming back to them. Perhaps they're still waiting.

'I don't even know what happened to Bainte, the White Horse of Legend. When Oisin fell, I was so busy looking at him that I never even saw the horse disappearing.

'Oisin lives still. He's the oldest man in Erin – in all the world. He lives peacefully in a monastery with Saint Patrick, where he tends the garden and grows herbs and healing plants.

'Oisin and I have spoken about that fateful day when he returned to Erin. I have asked him about the sword, and the lightning and the hand that rose up out of the water to take it.

'At first the old man would say nothing, but finally, when I persisted, he told me only that it would become a symbol for both nations, the Land of Erin and the Land of the Britons. The Gaels would know of it as the Cliamh Solas, the Sword of Light, and the Britons would come to call it Excalibur.'